Jill McDougall
Illustrations by Nives Porcellato and Andrew Craig

Contents

The Frozen North

What Is the Arctic?

The Arctic is the most northern part of Earth. It is a vast area of land and sea, almost as large as North America.

Many countries have part of their land in the Arctic. The northern edges of the continents of Asia, Europe and North America lie in the Arctic.

The Arctic Ocean, which is the smallest of Earth's oceans, makes up the rest of the Arctic.

The Arctic Circle

The Arctic Circle is an imaginary line that circles the globe. It is often used to mark the southern boundary of the Arctic. At the centre of the Arctic Circle is the North Pole – the most northern point on our planet.

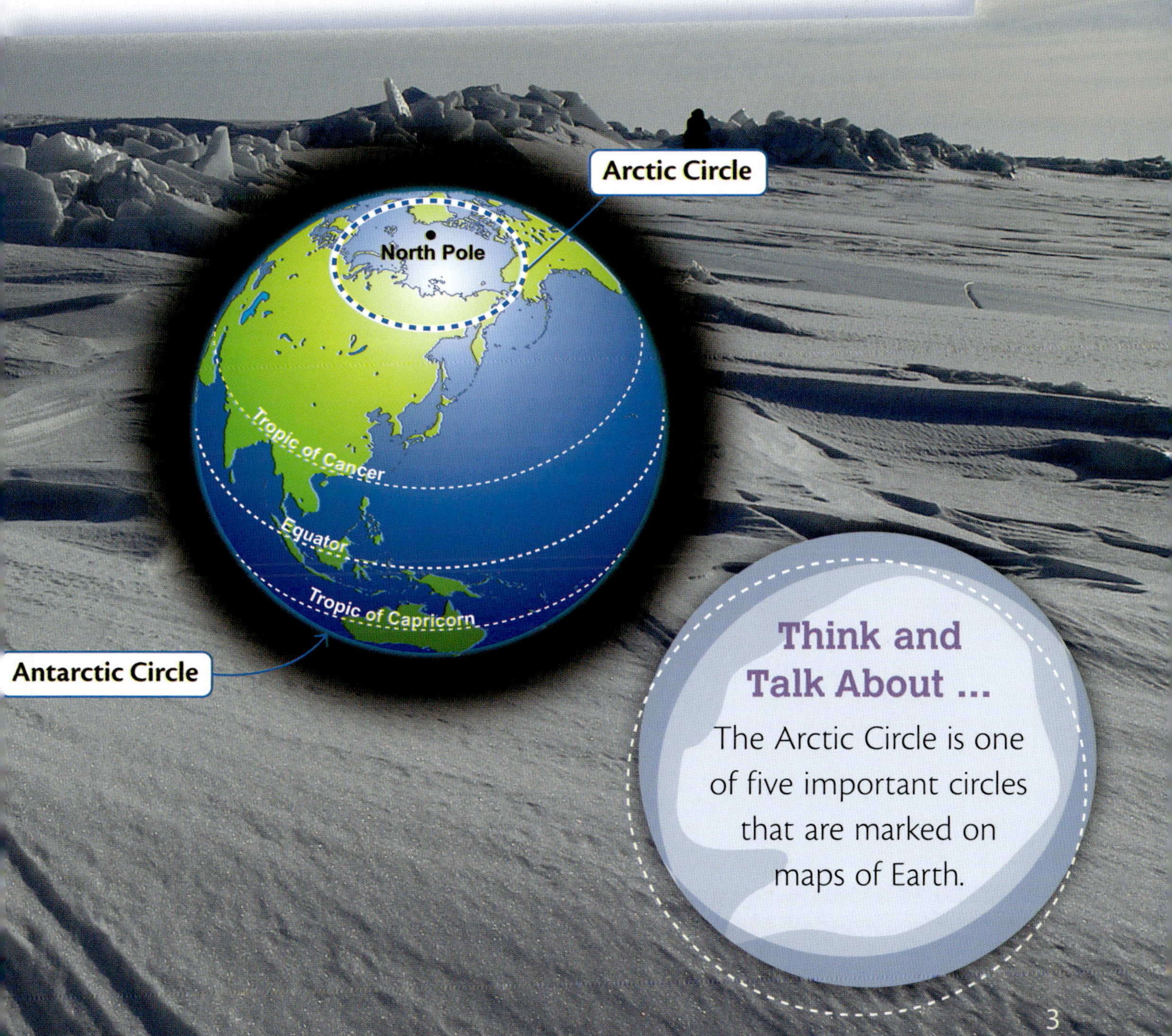

Think and Talk About ...

The Arctic Circle is one of five important circles that are marked on maps of Earth.

Arctic Geography

The Arctic is made up of an ocean surrounded by frozen land. There are treeless plains called **tundra**, small rounded hills and icy mountain peaks. The Arctic also contains many lakes and several of the world's biggest rivers.

Some parts of the Arctic are covered all year long with sheets of ice. Most of the country of Greenland is inside the Arctic Circle, and covered in a vast sheet of ice about 2400 kilometres long.

Greenland's ice sheet covers more than three quarters of the country.

Arctic Deserts

The Arctic is mostly very dry, as it gets little rain or other kinds of **precipitation**. Some parts of the Arctic are so dry they are called deserts, even though they are covered in snow and ice. They receive as little precipitation as the Sahara Desert! Most of the Arctic's precipitation is falling snow.

Snow falls over a forest in the southern part of the Arctic.

Arctic Seasons

In the winter months, most of the Arctic is cold and windy. The ground is covered with a thick layer of snow and ice, and the temperature is usually below freezing. Salt water does not usually freeze, but the Arctic Ocean gets so cold that a thick layer of ice forms on top of it.

Arctic summers are short and cool. When the snow begins to melt, the tundra become wet and boggy. The soil stays frozen, therefore water from the melting snow cannot drain into the ground. Instead, the melting snow collects on the surface, forming lakes and streams.

In spring, new streams form as the ice melts.

As the weather becomes warmer, most of the ice in the Arctic Ocean begins to break up into smaller chunks. Some of the ocean is open water, dotted with floating **icebergs**. However, in the central part of the Arctic Ocean, there is a huge pack of ice that stays frozen all year long.

The Land of the Midnight Sun

During the Arctic winter, there are months when the Sun is never above the horizon. This is because Earth is tilted away from the Sun. In summer, the Sun does not set, because Earth is tilted towards the Sun. For this reason, the Arctic is sometimes called "the land of the midnight Sun". The Sun can be shining at midnight!

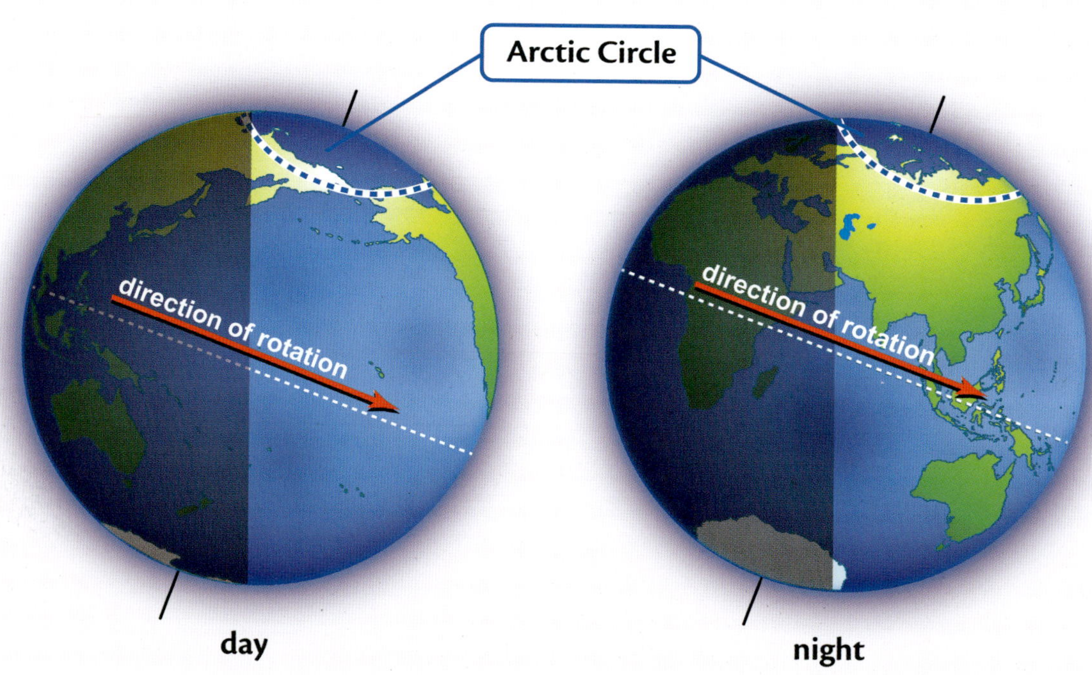

In summer, the Sun shines on the Arctic 24 hours a day.

Think and Talk About ...

The North Pole has only one sunrise and one sunset every year.

Arctic Plants

Plants in the Arctic must survive icy winds and freezing temperatures. There are forests in the southern parts of the Arctic, but further north much of the ground remains frozen all year long, so very few trees can grow. The frozen ground does not allow the tree roots to burrow deep enough.

Most plants in the Arctic grow low to the ground, where they can avoid the strong winds. During winter, plants such as grasses and low shrubs lie under a blanket of snow, their roots protected from the cold winds. As soon as the ice melts, they begin to grow again. **Lichen** is a type of plant that can keep growing, even under the snow.

Lichen can be seen when the snow melts away in summer.

Tundra become green in summer, when the snow melts.

Think and Talk About ...

In summer, the flowers of the Arctic poppy turn to face the Sun as it moves slowly across the sky.

Arctic Animals

Many different animals live in the Arctic. The ocean and waterways are teeming with fish of all kinds. Seals feed in the icy water and raise their young on the floating ice. Walruses live where the ice pack meets the open water. They dive for clams on the sea floor, then climb onto the ice to rest.

On land, there are several kinds of mammals, including wolves, polar bears, Arctic foxes, **musk oxen** and large deer called caribou. In summer, there are also many birds and hundreds of small insects, such as mosquitoes.

harp seals resting in the sunshine

White coats help Arctic wolves blend into the snow when they hunt.

Caribou travel in herds to keep them safer from predators such as wolves.

Think and Talk About ...

Caribou herds are always on the move, wandering between summer and winter feeding grounds.

Arctic Adaptations

Animals in the Arctic have many different ways to survive the Arctic winter. These are called adaptations. The small ground squirrel survives the long winters by **hibernating** beneath the snow. It lines its burrow with lichen and hairs from musk oxen, then it rolls into a ball and "sleeps" for seven months.

Other animals, such as the wolf and the Arctic fox, develop thick winter coats to protect them against the cold. The musk ox has long, shaggy hair that hangs down to the ground. Some birds grow dense, fluffy feathers and an extra layer of fat to keep out the cold.

In the freezing waters of the Arctic Ocean, sea animals, such as seals and walruses, are covered in thick layers of **blubber** that keep them warm.

Musk oxen grow long, thick coats for winter.

Arctic Adaptations of the Caribou

Arctic Migrants

There are many birds, and some mammals, that cannot survive in the Arctic winter. As the temperature begins to drop, they **migrate** south to warmer parts of the world. They do not return until the Arctic summer, when they come back to feed and build nests.

A small seabird, the Arctic tern, undertakes a migration every year from the Arctic to the Antarctic and back again. This is the longest migration of any animal in the world.

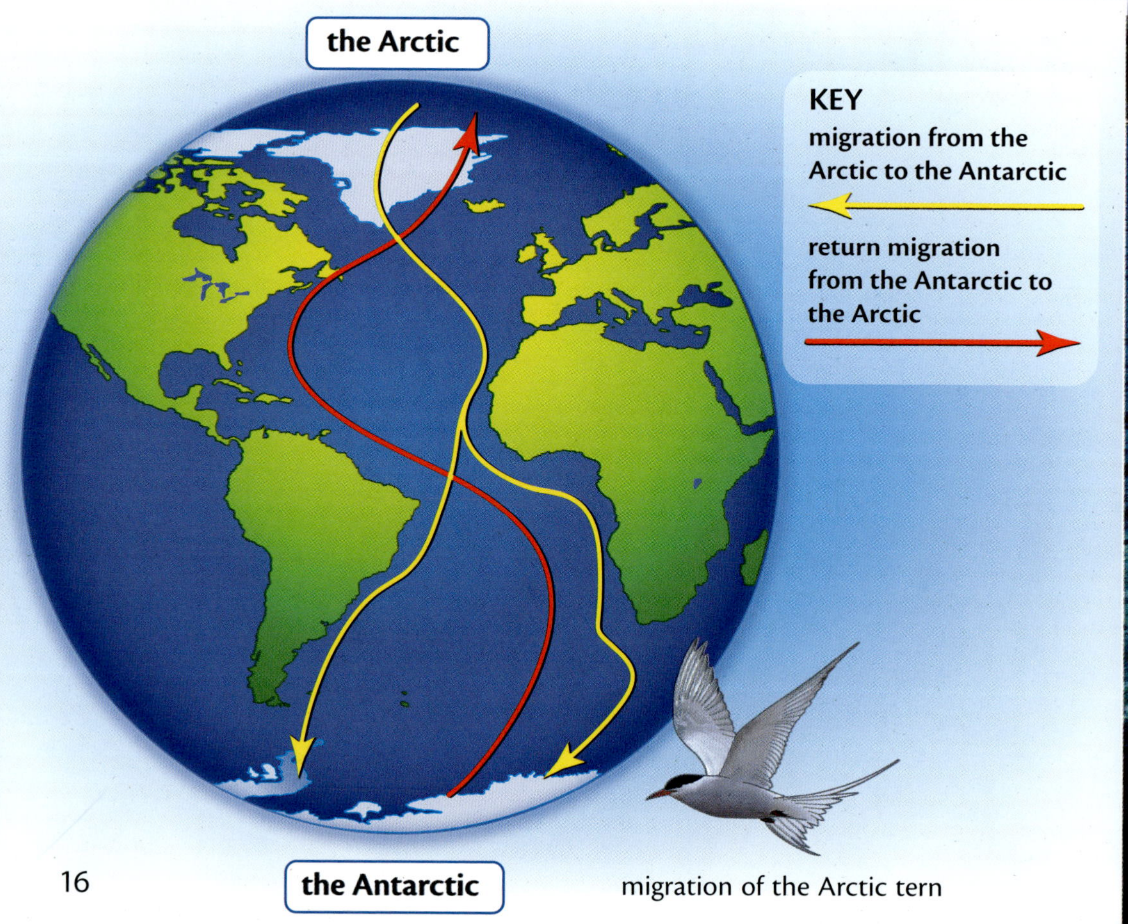

migration of the Arctic tern

Each year, grey whales migrate from Mexico to the Arctic. In the winter, they give birth to their young in the warm waters off the coast of Mexico, then travel north to the Arctic for the summer, when there is plenty of food in the Arctic Ocean.

Grey whales stay close to the coast throughout their migration.

Arctic Peoples

The Inuit (pronounced *IN-you-it*) and Aleut (*al-ee-OOT*) **indigenous** peoples have lived in and near the Arctic for thousands of years. They learned to survive in the harsh climate by hunting and gathering food, and making warm clothes from animal skins and fur. In parts of the Arctic, indigenous people still hunt animals such as caribou and whales.

Indigenous people invented **kayaks**, skis and **snowshoes** to help them travel in the Arctic. Today, snowmobiles are a more common means of transport across the ice, and speedboats are often used to travel across water.

Inuit women making clothes from the fur and skin of seals and caribou

Think and Talk About ...

Arctic indigenous people learned how to make use of every part of an animal's body.

Today, indigenous people of the Arctic prefer to travel by snowmobile.

Long ago, indigenous people built their houses out of materials such as animal hides, whale bone and snow. Today, most people in the Arctic live in houses that are similar to those found in many cities.

People in the north **traditionally** used the oil from the fat of seals or other sea mammals for lamps and fires.

Today, there are towns and cities in the Arctic with supermarkets, cinemas and even skate parks. However, many indigenous people strive to keep their culture strong by teaching their children the way of life of their **ancestors**.

An Inuit woman teaches her grandchildren to clean the fish she has caught.

the town of Ilulissat in Greenland

Arctic Resources

The Arctic has large amounts of natural resources, such as oil, gas, minerals and fish. For this reason, many nations around the world want to explore and develop the Arctic.

Oil companies build huge platforms in the Arctic Ocean to drill for oil.

Water is the Arctic's biggest resource. Twenty per cent of all Earth's water is frozen in Arctic ice and glaciers.

Glaciers are enormous rivers of very slowly moving ice.

Climate Change and the Arctic

In recent years, the climate on Earth has changed. It has become warmer, which means that the Arctic sea ice is melting at a faster rate than in the past. There is less ice on the ocean than ever before. This affects many animals that depend on sea ice to survive.

Polar bears roam across the floating packs of ice to hunt for seals. As the ice melts, the polar bears have smaller hunting grounds, and cannot always find enough food. Seals use the sea ice to raise their young, and walruses use the sea ice as a resting place after diving for food.

Summer Sea Ice in 1979 Compared to Today

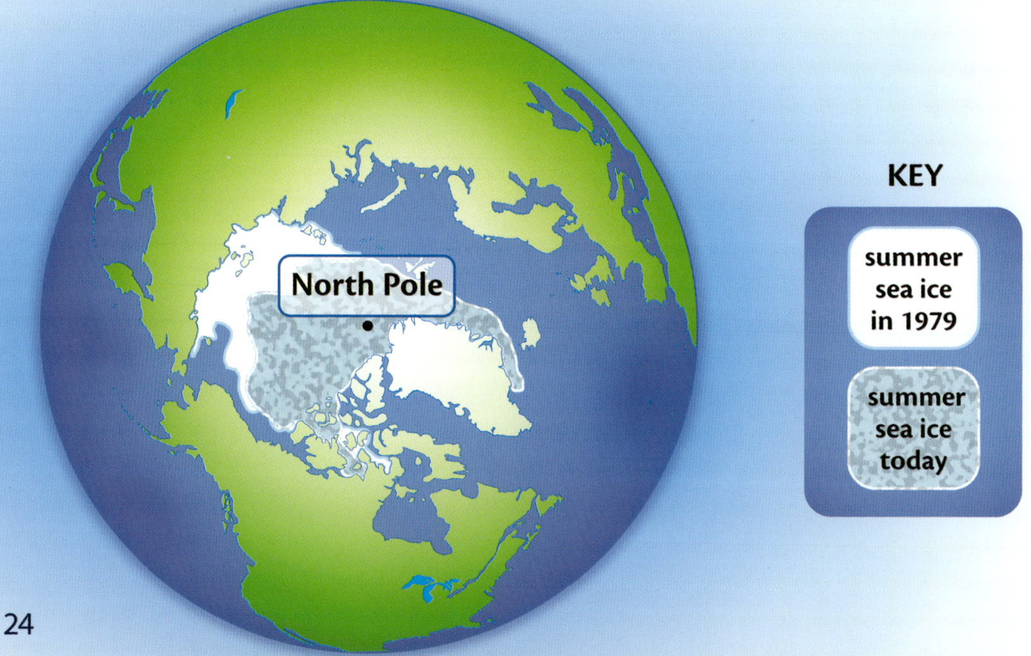

Walruses depend on the Arctic sea ice for a place to rest.

The melting of Arctic ice has an effect on the entire planet. The vast areas of ice at the Arctic help keep our planet cool. The bright white ice reflects the Sun's heat back into space. When there is less ice to reflect the heat away from Earth, the planet becomes warmer.

The ice on the land is also melting more quickly than ever before. The water from melting ice and snow rushes into rivers and into the ocean. Over time, this will lead to a rise in the level of the sea all around the world. Many low areas will become flooded and crops and homes could be destroyed.

Low-lying towns on the coast are in danger of being flooded as the sea level rises.

The Arctic is a unique and beautiful place, but also a harsh environment to live in. The people, animals and plants of the Arctic have many ways of surviving the extreme conditions there. The changing climate could be a greater threat than any other.

an Arctic hare sheltering from the wind

Think and Talk About ...

Most people in the world live along the coast.

SOS! Save the Polar Bears!

The polar bears are in danger, and we need to save them. Polar bears live near the Arctic Ocean, where their main food is seal meat. In winter, polar bears travel long distances across the sea ice to hunt for seals. However, Earth's climate is warming up and the sea ice is melting at a fast rate. Polar bears do not have as much time to hunt for seals before the ice melts.

Scientists tell us that if polar bears cannot find enough food to eat, they are in danger of becoming **extinct**.

People must remember that extinction is forever. Once the polar bears are gone, they are gone for good!

Take Action Now!

Polar bears are an important part of the food web in the Arctic Ocean. In a food web, many species depend on one another for survival. When one part of a food web is removed, the result can be a disaster!

If the polar bear disappeared from the Arctic, the seals would have fewer **predators**. There would be more seals living in the ocean, hunting for food. Seals feed on fish, so the fish would soon disappear.

The Arctic fox could also be in danger if polar bears became extinct. During the freezing cold winters, Arctic foxes eat the leftovers from a polar bear's kill. Without the polar bear, the Arctic fox could starve.

If the polar bear becomes extinct, other animals will, too. It is very important that we save the polar bear.

We need to take action now!

Arctic species all depend on each other for food.

Glossary

ancestors (*noun*)	all of the past members of a family
blubber (*noun*)	a thick layer of fat below the skin of some animals
climate change (*noun*)	the warming of Earth's climate
extinct (*adjective*)	having no living members of the species
hibernating (*verb*)	spending the winter in a sleep-like state
icebergs (*noun*)	floating masses of ice
indigenous (*adjective*)	belonging to a certain place or region
kayaks (*noun*)	light watercrafts used for hunting
lichen (*noun*)	(pronounced *lie-ken*) a kind of plant that grows like a crust on rocks and trees
migrate (*verb*)	to travel long distances to feed or breed
musk oxen (*noun*)	large, heavy wild oxen
predators (*noun*)	animals that eat particular other animals
precipitation (*noun*)	water from the atmosphere that falls to Earth's surface
snowshoes (*noun*)	wide, net-covered frames attached under the feet, for walking on top of deep snow
traditionally (*adverb*)	in a way that has been the same for a long time
tundra (*noun*)	treeless plains in the Arctic

Index